Professor Pitt Is a Nitwit!

Dan Gutman

Pictures by
Jim Paillot

HARPER
An Imprint of HarperCollinsPublishers

To Emma

My Weirdtastic School #3: Professor Pitt Is a Nitwit!
Text copyright © 2023 by Dan Gutman
Illustrations copyright © 2023 by Jim Paillot
All rights reserved. Printed in the United States of America.

Library of Congress Control Number: 2023933842
ISBN 978-0-06-320701-1 (pbk bdg) — ISBN 978-0-06-320702-8 (trade bdg)

Typography by Laura Mock
23 24 25 26 27 LBC 5 4 3 2 1
First Edition

Contents

Ms. Hannah Loves Garbage

My name is A.J. and I know what you're thinking. You're thinking about babysitting. I know, because that's what I'm thinking about.

I don't get it. Why would anybody want to sit on a baby? That's mean. You could hurt the baby. What did a baby ever do to *you*?

The point is, we were in Miss Banks's class the other day.

"I have an announcement to make," Miss Banks announced. "School is canceled for the rest of your lifetime."

WHAT?!

Everybody started yelling and screaming and hooting and hollering and freaking out.

"Just kidding," said Miss Banks. "Time is fun when you're having flies! Line up for art class."

Miss Banks pulls lots of pranks.

I hate art class. Why do we have to have art? If you ask me, drawing pictures is for little kids.

"Yay, I *love* art!" announced Andrea,

this annoying girl with curly brown hair.

Of *course* Andrea loves art. She loves everything I hate. She even takes art classes after school. Andrea takes classes in *everything* after school. If they gave classes in how to blow your nose, she would take that class so she could get better at it.

Andrea took a big box out of her desk. It had crayons, colored pencils, glue sticks, and other artsy stuff in it.

"When I grow up, I want to be an artist," Andrea said. "My mom thinks I'm really creative. I like to make things."

"She should make like a tree and leave," I whispered to Michael, who never ties his shoes.

Michael laughed, but Miss Banks made a mean face at him and he stopped laughing really fast.

"Any questions before we head to the art room?" asked Miss Banks.

"If you add an F to ART you get fart," I said.

Everybody laughed because I said "fart." Anytime anybody says the word "fart," you have to laugh. That's the first rule of being a kid.

"That's not a question, A.J.," said Miss

Banks. "But thank you for that valuable insight. Onward, fourth graders! To the art room!"

The art room is on the other side of the school. We had to walk a million hundred miles to get there. Ryan, who will eat anything, was the door holder. Alexia, this girl who rides a skateboard all the time, was the line leader.

Our art teacher, Ms. Hannah, was already waiting for

us outside the art room. She was wearing a weird hat.

"Good morning, fourth graders!" she said as we filed into the art room. "Do you like my new hat? I made it from bottle caps I found in the garbage can next to the vending machine in the teachers' lounge."

It was the weirdest-looking hat in the history of the world. But I didn't say that, because it would be rude.

"Your hat is *bee-you-tee-full*!" Andrea gushed.

"I agree!" said Andrea's crybaby friend, Emily, who always agrees with Andrea.

Ms. Hannah could have made her hat out of frog turds and Andrea and Emily would say it was beautiful. Those two love sucking up to teachers.

The art room is filled with all kinds of junk—old musical instruments, broken toys, bubble wrap, plastic bags, clothespins. At home, my mom makes me clean up my room all the time and pick up after myself. But I guess art teachers are allowed to be slobs.

Hey, maybe I should become an art teacher when I grow up!

Neil, who we call the nude kid even though he wears clothes, asked Ms. Hannah where he could throw away his gum.

"Oh, I don't have a garbage can," she said as she took Neil's gum and put it in a jar that said OLD GUM on it. "I *love* garbage.

In fact, on garbage day, the garbage men bring the garbage to *me*. I feel sad when people throw things away."

Ms. Hannah is bananas. One time, I blew my nose into a tissue, and Ms. Hannah stuck the tissue to a big ball of paper the size of a beach ball. It was gross.

"Today, we're going to do something different," she announced.

Uh-oh. I didn't like the sound of that. Different is scary.

"A special guest has come to speak to us," said Ms. Hannah. "I'd like to introduce you to my old art history teacher. He's also the president of the Museum of Recent Art, the esteemed Professor

Armand Pitt."*

Armand Pitt? I bet when he was a kid, all the other kids called him "armpit." How could you not?

We all clapped because that's what you're supposed to do when people get introduced, even if they didn't do anything yet.

This guy walked into the room. He had long hair, was dressed in all black, and was wearing a cape. I always thought that only superheroes, like my third-grade teacher, Mr. Cooper, could wear capes. But I guess anybody is allowed to wear one. Oh, and Professor Armpit was wearing a beret, which is sort of like a Frisbee made

---

*Why would you steam a professor? Isn't that dangerous?

out of cloth that you put on your head.

"*Bonjour,*" said Professor Armpit, and he took a big bow.

That means "hello" in French. I know lots of French. Like, if you want to say "yes," you say "*oui.*" But it's pronounced "we," which makes no sense at all.

Well, I guess that's all the French I know. But you can really communicate a lot by just saying "hello" and "yes."

"The professor is going to talk to us about art history," said Ms. Hannah. "Isn't that exciting?"

"Yes!" shouted all the girls.

"No!" shouted all the boys.

Art history? Was she kidding? Art is boring. History is boring. So art history must be *super* boring.

"Art is how we express creativity," said Professor Armpit. *"Blah blah blah blah* feelings *blah blah blah blah* meaning *blah blah blah blah* color and shape *blah blah blah blah."* What's he talking about? *"Blah blah blah blah."* When is it going to end? *"Blah blah blah blah."* I'm getting sleepy. *"Blah blah blah blah."* What's for lunch? *"Blah blah blah blah."* Why do people sit on babies? *"Blah blah. . . ."* Zzzzzzzzzzzzzzzz.

Anything Can Be Art

Oh, sorry. I must have dozed off in the middle of Professor Armpit's fascinating talk about . . . whatever he was talking about. What a snoozefest.

When I woke up, Professor Armpit was gone. At least I wouldn't have to listen to him talk anymore.

But I was wrong.

The next morning, after we pledged the allegiance, Miss Banks announced, "Instead of math and social studies today, we're going on a field trip!"

At first, I thought she was just pulling another one of her pranks, but she insisted she was serious. We were really going on a field trip.

"Field trip!" yelled Alexia.

"Field trip!" yelled Neil.

"Field trip!" yelled Ryan.

Everybody started yelling "field trip!"

Field trips are cool. Well, except for field trips to a field. Those field trips are boring.

"Where are we going?" asked Andrea, the Human Homework Machine.

"We're taking a tour of a radioactive

toxic waste dump," replied Miss Banks.

WHAT?!

"Just kidding," she said. "We're going to the Museum of Recent Art. Professor Pitt invited us to be his guests."

"Yay!" shouted Andrea. "I love museums!"

Ugh, I hate museums. Museums are boring. I would rather have hot needles poked into my eyes than look at a bunch of dumb paintings.

But Miss Banks said we had to go. We walked single file to the front door of the school, where the bus was waiting.

"Bingle boo!" said our bus driver, Mrs. Kormel.

Mrs. Kormel is not normal. She invented her own secret language. It's sort of like

French. "Bingle boo" means "hello."

"How come we never go on a field trip to a skateboard museum?" I complained to Ryan as we climbed on the bus.

"Because there's no such thing as a skateboard museum," he replied.

Well, there *should* be.

"Museums are fun!" said Andrea, who sat across the aisle from me. "My mom has been taking me to museums for years."

"For years?" I asked. "Don't they close museums at the end of each day?" Andrea just rolled her eyes.

When we arrived at the Museum of Recent Art, we had to climb up a million hundred steps. What's up with that? Why do museums have so many steps in front of them? They should put museums at ground level, like normal buildings.

Anyway, you'll never believe who was waiting for us at the top of the steps.

It was Ms. Hannah!

"I hope you kids are excited," she said as she led us inside the museum. "Within these walls are the greatest works of art of the last hundred years."

"WOW," everybody said, which is "MOM" upside down.

Maybe going to the museum wouldn't be so bad. At least we didn't have to learn math or social studies.

Ms. Hannah led us down a hallway until she found Professor Armpit's office.

"*Bonjour*!" he said. "Welcome to the Museum of Recent Art. Before we get started on our tour, are there any questions?"

"Can we go to the gift shop?" asked Michael.

"Maybe later," said Professor Armpit.

Gift shops are cool. They have all kinds of useful stuff, like refrigerator magnets and souvenir spoons with your name on them. If you ask me, I'd rather go to a museum gift shop than go to a museum.

"Any other questions?" asked Professor Armpit.

"Yeah," I said. "What's the capital of France?"

"Uh, Paris," said Professor Armpit. "Why do you ask?"

"I just want to make sure you're really French," I told him. "What's your favorite French food?"

"French fries," he replied.

"Well, okay," I said. "Maybe you really are French."

"Come," Professor Armpit told us, "I want to show you some treasures of our collection."

We followed him to a big room filled with all kinds of weird art. One painting was a bunch of black lines on a gray background. Another one was a bunch of gray lines on a black background. In the middle of the room was one of those kinetic sculptures from Connecticut that turn around for no reason.

Professor Armpit stopped in front of a painting that had a big blob of red on top of a big blob of green. It was called *Summer in Hoboken*.

"Look at this!" Professor Armpit said. "Isn't it marvelous?"

"I don't get it," I admitted.

"Open your imagination," said Professor Armpit. "Everything in the world is beautiful. Art is everything and everywhere! And art changes the world."

"Can we go to the gift shop now?" asked Neil.

"Not right now," said Ms. Hannah.

Professor Armpit stopped in front of a giant painting with purple blotches all over it.

"What do you see here?" he asked.

"It looks like somebody tripped over a can of paint and made a big mess," I said.

"It's called *Maximum Cardboard Bicycle Magic*," Ms. Hannah said as she read a little note on the wall next to the dumb painting.

Huh?

"It's *bee-you-tee-full*!" said Andrea and Emily, who think any art is beautiful as long as it's in a museum.

"Look at this!" said Professor Armpit. "Isn't it marvelous?"

He was pointing at the corner of the room. There was a bucket of water with a mop next to it.

"The janitor must be in the middle of

cleaning up," I said.

"Actually, this is a sculpture," Professor Armpit told me. "The artist is making a comment about water pollution killing fish in the ocean. This piece of art is worth over a million dollars."

"You *gotta* be kidding me," mumbled Michael.

"You see?" said Professor Armpit. "Art is

all around us! We are all artists, in a way."

"Can kids be artists?" asked Andrea. "Can *I* be an artist?"

"Of course," said Professor Armpit.

"I wouldn't want to be an artist," I said. "This stuff is dumb."

"Well," said Professor Armpit, "art is in the eye of beholder."

Huh? Why would a bee holder know anything about art?*

"Can we go to the gift shop now?" asked Alexia.

"No!" shouted Ms. Hannah.

"*Blah blah blah* masterpiece," said Professor Armpit. "*Blah blah blah* parallel lines

---

*Why would anybody want to hold bees, anyway? You might get stung.

23

blah blah blah flowing shapes *blah blah blah* forms *blah blah blah* deep meanings *blah blah blah* brushwork *blah blah blah* composition *blah blah blah* light *blah blah blah* . . ."

I wanted to run away to Antarctica and go live with the penguins.

We walked around the museum for a million hundred hours. I thought I was gonna die from boredom. Get me outta here! I was hungry and my feet were tired.

Finally, it was time to go, and we got back on the bus. We never did get to go to the gift shop. Next time, I hope we go on a field trip to a field.

The Greatest Idea in the History of the World

When we got back to school, Ms. Hannah brought us to the junk room. I mean, the art room.

"I hope visiting the Museum of Recent Art inspired you to create some art of your own," she said. "Let's do finger painting!"

Ugh. No way.

"I'm not gonna paint my fingers," I said.

Everybody laughed even though I didn't say anything funny.

"No, silly!" Ms. Hannah told me as she took some tubes of paint out of the closet. "You use your fingers like a paintbrush."

"What should we paint?" asked Emily.

"Anything you like!" replied Ms. Hannah.

"Express your creativity. Just paint what you love."

"I love flowers," Andrea said. "I'm going to make a pretty picture of roses in a colorful garden."

"I'm going to make a barn next to Andrea's rose garden," said Emily.

"I'm going to make a picture of a hurricane," I said, "blowing down a barn and crushing a garden full of roses."

Andrea rolled her eyes.

"That's mean!" Emily said. She looked like she was going to cry, as usual.

"Hey, I'm just expressing my creativity," I told her.

Everybody got to work. Ryan started finger painting a picture of a car. Michael started finger painting a picture of a football. Everybody was hard at work finger painting.

I didn't want to get that yucky finger paint all over my hands. It was gross. I just sat there watching everybody.

Ms. Hannah walked around the room looking at everybody's artwork.

"That's very nice, Andrea," she said.

"That's lovely, Neil," she said.

"Very interesting, Alexia," she said.

Grown-ups say "very interesting" when something is terrible but they don't want to hurt a kid's feelings. I'm on to their tricks.

"A.J.," whispered Emily, "why aren't you finger painting?"

"None of your beeswax," I told her.

"Ms. Hannah!" Andrea called out. "A.J. isn't finger painting."

Why can't a truck full of finger paint fall on tattletale Andrea's head? She stuck out her tongue at me as Ms. Hannah came over to my table.

"Is anything wrong, A.J.?" Ms. Hannah asked. "Don't you want to create some artwork?"

"No," I said. "I'm not artistic."

Ms. Hannah laughed. "Oh, come on! Remember what Professor Pitt told us. *Everyone* is artistic. Let's go, A.J. This period is almost over. I want to see you make some art before the bell rings."

Ms. Hannah walked away. I looked at

the clock. There were five minutes left in the period. How was I supposed to make art in just five minutes? I didn't have any ideas.

Four minutes.

Three minutes.

Two minutes. I didn't know what to say. I didn't know what to do. I had to think fast.

That's when I came up with the greatest idea in the history of the world.

I picked up a tube of finger paint. Then I tore off a long piece of Scotch tape from the tape dispenser.

"What are you doing, A.J.?" asked Emily.

"You'll see."

I stuck the strip of tape to the tube of finger paint. Then I got up and taped the tube against the wall.

"There!" I announced. "That's my art."

Everybody laughed.

"That's not art!" said Andrea. "You just taped a tube of paint to the wall."

"Yeah, I know," I said. "Art is in the eye of the bee holder."

"It is not!"

"Is too!"

"Ooooooooooh," said Ryan. "A.J. and Andrea are bickering. They must be in *love*!"

"When are you gonna get married?" asked Michael.

"Settle down, kids," said Ms. Hannah.

"Admit it, Arlo," whispered Andrea. "You're just too lazy to paint a picture."

"Hey," I told Andrea, "Professor Armpit said anything can be art. This is a thing, so it's art."

"Says who?"

"Says me!" I shouted at her. "They had a bucket and a mop in the museum that's worth a million dollars. If that's art, I say a tube of paint taped to the wall is art too."

"It is not!"

"Is too!"

We went on like that for a while, until ...

*Brrrrriiiiiinnnnnggggg!**

The bell rang. Art class was over. It was time to go to lunch.

But you'll never believe who walked into the door at that moment.

Nobody! Why would somebody walk into a door? You could break your nose.

---

*Bells go *brrrrriiiiiinnnnnggggg*. Nobody knows why.

But you'll never believe who walked into the door*way*.

I'm not going to tell you.

Okay, okay, I'll tell you. But you have to read the next chapter. So nah-nah-nah boo-boo on you!

Art of the Future

It was Professor Armpit!

"*Bonjour*!" he announced as he glided into the room. "I was just in the neighborhood, so I thought I'd stop by to say *bonjour.*"

"*Bonjour*!" we all said.

"You're always welcome in my art room, Professor," said Ms. Hannah. "The children were really inspired by our visit to the museum. Would you like to take a look at the art our talented students are creating?"

"Certainly!"

"Uh-oh," Ryan whispered to me. "You're in trouble, dude."

Professor Armpit walked around the room, stopping at each desk to look at what each kid made. He went to Andrea's desk first, of course.

"Hmmmmm," he said as he looked at Andrea's dumb picture of flowers.

Grown-ups always say "hmmmmm"

when they don't know what to say.

"Very interesting," Professor Armpit finally said to Andrea. Then he went to Emily's desk.

"Very interesting," he said. Then he went to Michael's desk.

"Very interesting," he said. Then he went to Neil's desk.

"Very interesting," he said.

Professor Armpit said everybody's art was very interesting.* Finally, he came over to me. He looked at my desk.

"No art, young man?" he asked.

I pointed up at the wall next to me.

Professor Armpit looked at my tube of

---

*Wow, he must really hate it.

paint taped to the wall. Then he walked back and forth so he could look at it from different angles. He stared at it for like a million hundred minutes.

"Hmmmmm . . ." he said.

You never know what "hmmmmm" means. "Hmmmmm" could be good or "hmmmmm" could be bad.

"What do you call this, young man?" Professor Armpit finally asked.

Call it? How should I know? I didn't even know that art had names.

Everybody was looking at me. Nobody said anything. You could have heard a pin drop. That is, if anybody brought pins with them to school. But that would make no sense at all.

I didn't know what to say. I didn't know what to do. I had to think fast.

"Uh . . . I call it Future Art," I finally said.

"Hmmmmm . . ." said Professor Armpit.

"Future Art?"

"Yeah," I told him. "It's not art yet, because the paint is still in the tube. But it could be art someday . . . in the future."

Professor Armpit stuck his face really close to the tube of paint I taped to the wall. He stared at it for a long time.

"Art of the future?" he finally said. And then he shouted, "IT'S GENIUS!"

Artlo

I thought Professor Armpit had to be joking. I didn't make any art. All I did was tape a tube of paint to the wall. And he fell for it. What a scam.

"YES! YES! YES!" Professor Armpit shouted. "This young man is a genius!"

I looked over at Andrea. She had on

her mean face, and her arms were folded in front of her. Anytime somebody folds their arms in front of them, it means they're mad. Nobody knows why. I stuck my tongue out at Andrea.

"Well, yes," said Ms. Hannah, "all of our students at Ella Mentry School are creative. I work very hard every day to encourage them to—"

"He is *brilliant*!" interrupted Professor Armpit. "This is a masterpiece that combines the elements of post-modernist *blah blah blah blah* with new wave expressionism *blah blah blah blah*..."

He went on and on about my fake art. Professor Armpit was so excited. I thought he was gonna faint.

"All he did was tape a tube of paint to the wall!" shouted Andrea.

Boy, was she mad! It was the greatest moment of my life. This was the next best thing to watching an elephant fall on Andrea's head.

"What's the big deal?" asked Alexia. "*Any* of us could have done that."

"But none of you *did*!" said Professor Armpit. "Don't you see? The tube of paint is symbolic of the future *blah blah blah blah*, and the tape symbolizes the shackles we have that prevent humanity from achieving our dreams of a perfect future *blah blah blah blah*."

"Yeah," I added. "What he said."

"Do you like my flowers?" asked Andrea. But Professor Armpit just ignored her. He couldn't take his eyes off the paint tube I taped to the wall.

"I have not been this excited about a new young artist since Keith Haring came on the scene," said Professor Armpit.

I had no idea who that guy was.

"You are going to be the next big thing!" he continued. "The next Van Gogh! The next Rembrandt! The next Picasso!"

"Who are they?" asked Neil.

"I think they used to play for the Lakers," I told him.

Andrea was really mad.

"It's not fair!" she said, stomping her foot on the floor. "Arlo isn't an artist! He's never even heard of Picasso!"

Professor Armpit stuck his face near mine.

"Your name is Arlo?" he asked.

"Yeah," I admitted. The only person who calls me Arlo is Andrea, because she knows I don't like it.

"From now on," Professor Armpit said, "the world will know you as . . . Artlo!"

"Artlo?" I asked.

"Yes, the great artists of history were

known by one name—Michelangelo, Leon-
ardo, Raphael . . ."*

Professor Armpit couldn't stop raving
about my dumb artwork.

"I've been waiting my entire life to dis-
cover the next genius," he said. "And here
I have discovered Artlo, in the least likely
place."

"You can call me A.J.," I told him.

"It's funny, Artlo," said Professor Armpit. "Sometimes we can spend our lives
searching for something, and the whole
time it was right under our nose."

What was he talking about? Right under

---

*I didn't know the Teenage Mutant Ninja Turtles were art-
ists.

my nose is my mouth.

Professor Armpit grabbed my hands.

"Artlo, allow me to touch the hands that created this masterpiece," he said. "Let me touch the brain that could think such thoughts."

"Hey, don't mess with the hair, dude," I told him.

Professor Armpit is a nitwit!

The Next Picasso

I thought that would be the end of it. We went back to class and did math, social studies, and reading with Miss Banks. Then it was time for dismissal, and I took the bus home. Everything was normal.

It was almost time for dinner. That's when the weirdest thing in the history of the world happened.

The doorbell rang.

Well, that's not the weird part. Door-
bells ring all the time. The weird part was
what happened after *that*.

I looked through the little peephole
in the door. And do you know who was
standing on our front steps? It was Professor Armpit! I opened the door.

"Artlo!" he said.

"What are you doing here?" I asked
him.

"I have come to introduce you to the art
world!" he said dramatically.

"Uh, I have homework . . ."

"Homework can wait!" Professor Armpit
said.

Sounded good to me. I hate doing home-work.

At that point, my parents came in from the kitchen.

"Did I hear the doorbell ring?" my mother asked.

"I'm here to talk about your son," said Professor Armpit.

"What did he do *now*?" asked my mom.

"Has he been kicked out of school?" asked my dad.

"No!" Professor Armpit said with a laugh. "I'm Professor Pitt from the Museum of Recent Art. Your son has created the most groundbreaking sculpture I've seen in years. He's an artistic genius!"

51

"Are you sure you have the right address?" asked my dad.

"*Blah blah blah blah* the next big thing," said Professor Armpit. "*Blah blah blah blah* prodigy *blah blah blah blah* once in a lifetime *blah blah blah blah* . . ."

Somehow, Professor Armpit convinced my parents that I was the next Picasso. He said he wanted to take us to a party in my honor at an art gallery.

"We were about to sit down for dinner," my dad said.

"A.J. is an artist?" said my mom, getting her coat. "*This* I gotta see. Dinner can wait. Let's go!"

We drove a million hundred miles until

we got to the art gallery. I said I was hungry, and Professor Armpit told me the gallery would have some things called "oar derves," whatever they are.

As soon as we walked inside, I could see the gallery was filled with a bunch of art nerds like Professor Armpit, wearing capes and berets. Everybody burst into applause when I came into the room.

My dumb paint tube was taped to a white wall. And do you know what was on the table?

A bowl of pretzels!

I made a beeline for the pretzels and stuffed my face.

"Attention, art lovers!" announced Professor Armpit.

Everybody got quiet.

"I'd like to introduce you to Artlo, the young genius I told you about."

"Well, if the esteemed Professor Pitt says the boy is a genius," some guy said, "it must be true."

"Speech! Speech!" somebody shouted. "Let the young genius speak!"

Everybody was staring at me. I wanted to run away to Antarctica and go live with the penguins.

"Uh . . . *Bonjour*!" I said.

Then I went over and whispered into Professor Armpit's ear, "I don't know what to say!"

"Don't worry," he whispered back. "I'll do the talking."

Then he said, "Ladies and gentlemen, Artlo only speaks French. But I think I can translate his artistic vision into English. Artlo has created this amazing sculpture. We don't know what it is yet. It can be *anything*. He calls it Future Art, because it is the future of art. We may not have a perfect future. It depends on what the artist creates with the paint in the tube. Is

that what you had in mind, Artlo?"

"*Oui*!" I said.

"He's the next Andy Warhol," said Professor Armpit. "*Blah blah blah blah* up-and-coming *blah blah blah blah* the next big thing *blah blah blah blah . . .*"

"I think Future Art is simply marvelous!" some lady said.

"I love it!" shouted somebody else.

"It would look perfect in my living room!"

"How much will you sell it for, Artlo?"

"Uh," I said, "a doll—"

I didn't have the chance to finish my sentence, because Professor Armpit clapped his hand over my mouth.

"We can discuss the price later," he said.

"For now, let's have a toast!"

Toast? I don't even like toast. I wanted more pretzels.

"To Artlo!" somebody shouted, raising a glass in the air.

Everybody raised a glass in the air.*

"To Artlo!" everybody else shouted. I didn't see any toast anywhere.

Professor Armpit leaned down and whispered in my ear, "Go mingle. But don't say anything."

A swarm of smiling art nerds surrounded me.

"So you're the young man everyone's talking about," a lady said.

---

*Where did they all get glasses? Do art nerds carry them around all day?

"*Oui!*" I replied. "*Bonjour.*"

"Young man," said an old man, "I think you are brilliant. How did you come up with this revolutionary idea?"

"Uh . . . " I replied. "*Oui!*"

"What will be your next creation?" somebody asked.

"*Oui!*" I replied. "*Bonjour.*"

This place was boring. I wanted more snacks. I walked around until I found my

parents chit-chatting with some art nerds.

"When did you first realize that your son was a gifted genius?" some lady asked.

"About ten minutes ago," my mother replied.

The party went on for a million hundred hours. What a snoozefest. I thought I was gonna die.

But then, I spotted something in the far corner of the room, on a table. It was a big bowl with orange stuff in it.

Cheez Doodles.

I *love* Cheez Doodles! I went over to the bowl and reached inside to get some. But before I could touch a Cheez Doodle, some art nerd grabbed my hand.

"What are you doing?" she shouted.

"I'm getting Cheez Doodles."

"Those aren't Cheez Doodles!" she hollered at me. "This is a priceless sculpture!"

Oh.

Sheesh. It sure looked like a bowl of Cheez Doodles to me. That lady needs to chillax.

7

Going Once . . .
Going Twice . . .

I was at school the next day, minding my own business in Miss Banks's class.

"Turn to page twenty-three in your math books," said Miss Banks.

Ugh. Do we *have* to do math? But that's when the weirdest thing in the history of the world happened. An announcement came over the loudspeaker.

Well, that's not the weird part. We get announcements over the loudspeaker all the time. The weird part was what happened next.

"Miss Banks, please send A.J. to the office."

"Ooooh!" everybody oooohed. "A.J. is in *trouble!*"

I got out of my seat and walked a million hundred miles to the office. And you'll never believe who was standing there.

I'm not going to tell you.

Okay, okay, I'll tell you. It was Professor Armpit!

"Artlo!" he said. "Quickly! I need you to

come with me."

"But it's the middle of a school day," I said.

"You can go to school *anytime,*" he told me. "This is a once-in-a-lifetime opportunity. Don't worry. I got permission from your parents."

Sounded good to me. At least I would be getting out of math.

We got into Professor Armpit's car and he drove downtown to some building with a sign that said CHRISTIE'S.

"What's this?" I asked. "A restaurant?"

"No."

We took the elevator to the second floor. It opened into a big room full of grown-ups sitting on chairs. There must have been a hundred of them, and they were all holding paddles in their hands.

"What's with the paddles?" I asked Professor Armpit. "Is this a Ping-Pong tournament?"

"No, it's an auction," he whispered. "We're going to sell your masterpiece. *Shhh!* Let's sit down."

We found seats in the back. I looked around the room. There were no pretzels or snacks anywhere.

"Nobody's gonna buy Future Art," I whispered to Professor Armpit.

"Sure they will," he whispered back. "Everything has its price."

In the front of the room, some guy in a suit was standing behind a podium. My dumb tube of paint was taped to the wall behind him.

"Our next artwork is by a young man who goes by the name of Artlo," he said into a microphone. "It is titled Future Art. Let's start the bidding. Who will offer one hundred dollars for this sculpture?"

A hundred dollars? Was he joking? It was a tube of paint taped to the wall!

A bunch of art nerds raised their paddles and shouted "A hundred!"

"Excellent start!" said the auctioneer. "Who will offer *two* hundred dollars?"

"Two hundred!" somebody shouted, raising his paddle.

"See?" Professor Armpit whispered. "Your art is valuable!"

"Do I hear three hundred dollars?" asked the auctioneer.

"Three hundred!" somebody yelled.

"Four hundred!"

"Five hundred!"

I couldn't believe it. These art nerds were bidding on my fake art!

"Six hundred!"

"Seven hundred!"

"Eight hundred!"

People were jumping out of their seats and holding their paddles in the air to get the auctioneer's attention. It was *amazing*. You should have been there!

"Nine hundred!"

"Nine fifty!"

"Nine seventy-five!"

"We have a bid for nine hundred and seventy-five dollars!" shouted the auctioneer. "Can we get a thousand?"

It was quiet for a minute. A bunch of art nerds were shooting glances at each other.

"Going once . . . going twice . . ." the auctioneer shouted.

A lady in a blue dress stood up and yelled, "I bid a thousand dollars!"

"Gasp!" everybody gasped.

"Sold!" shouted the auctioneer. "To the lady in the blue dress! For one thousand dollars!"

WHAT?! A thousand dollars? That's almost a million!

Everybody clapped. Professor Armpit said we should get out of there before anybody recognized me.

"This is just the *beginning*, Artlo," he said excitedly as we left the building. "That woman got a great deal! Very soon your art will be worth *thousands* of dollars. Maybe *millions*!"

"Bazillions?" I asked.*

"Maybe," Professor Armpit said.

Cool! I was going to be a bazillionaire!

---

*I'm not sure if "bazillion" is a real amount of money.

Parents Are Weird

As Professor Armpit drove me back to school, I thought about what I could do with a thousand dollars.

I could buy a speedboat. Yeah, that would be cool! But I don't think I'm old enough to drive a speedboat.

Maybe I could go to outer space! All

these bazillionaires are starting companies that send regular people to space. I could buy a ticket and be the first kid in space! Andrea would be *so* jealous.

Better yet, I thought, maybe I could just buy the Super Bowl! Yeah! I would rename it the Super Artlo Bowl.*

I was thinking so hard about what I was going to do with the money that I didn't notice Professor Armpit missed the turn to go back to school. He was driving to my house instead.

"Aren't you going to take me back to school?" I asked.

"Going to school will only hold back

---

*How cool would that be?

your genius," Professor Armpit told me as we pulled into my driveway.

"You mean I don't have to go to school anymore?" I asked.

"Of course not," he replied. "Your mind needs to be free to create your artistic vision."

Yay! No more school! This was the greatest day of my life.

I was about to get out of the car when Professor Armpit leaned over to me.

"I have an assignment for you, Artlo," he said. "The art world moves fast, and word gets around. You need to make twenty more pieces of art, as quickly as possible. We'll have a one-man show, fill a gallery with your new creations, and it will sell for millions. Can you do that?"

"Uh . . . okay," I replied.

At that moment, my parents came out of the house.

"How did the auction go?" asked my dad.

"My dumb sculpture sold for a thousand

dollars!" I told him.

"WHAT?!" shouted my mom. "A thousand dollars! That is *fantastic!*"

"And that's just the beginning," Professor Armpit told them. "Artlo is going to have his own one-man show. I'm sure the art will bring in *millions.*"

"Bazillions!" I said.

"That is great news!" my mom said excitedly. "This could pay for your college education, A.J.!"

"We could get a new car!" shouted my dad.

"Maybe we can build that swimming pool we've been talking about!" shouted my mom. "And, honey, you could retire early!"

WHAT?! I thought it was *my* money.

"I was thinking about buying the Super Bowl," I told them.

But my parents didn't hear me. They were jumping up and down and hugging each other.

"We can put a new addition on the house!" shouted my dad.

While they were celebrating, Professor Armpit whispered to me again.

"I've got to go," he said. "But this is very important, Artlo. Don't tell *anybody* about the new art you're working on. The art world is very competitive and secretive. There are spies *everywhere*. You don't want anybody to steal your genius ideas."

"Got it."

Professor Armpit reminded me to get to work on my new art right away. I got out of the car and he drove off. My parents finally calmed down. Dad had to go back to work, but my mom went into the house with me.

"Can I get you anything, sweetie?" she said. "Hot chocolate? A pillow? Some milk and cookies maybe?"

Boy, she was treating me awfully nice all of the sudden.

"Yeah," I replied. "Milk and cookies sounds good."

She went to get the milk and cookies while I lay on the couch.

"You rest," she hollered from the kitchen, "and think of all those great ideas that are floating around in your head."

Oh, yeah. Ideas. I didn't have any ideas. What could I create?

I thought and thought and thought. I thought so hard that I thought my head might split in half. My mind was blank. I guess I only come up with great ideas when I'm at school, where I can annoy

Andrea or make my friends laugh.

A few minutes later, Mom brought over a glass of milk and a plate full of chocolate chip cookies.

"Um, Mom," I said, "can I go back to school?"

"What?" my mother said as she put her hand against my forehead. "*You* want to go to school? I think you have a temperature, A.J. Are you feeling okay? Can I get you anything, sweetie?"

I looked at the clock on the wall. It was almost three o'clock. School would be letting out any minute. That's when I got the greatest idea in the history of the world.

"Can you go to the store and get me

some ice cream, Mom?" I asked. "And cake?"

"Of course!" she replied. "Anything for my little artist. I need to do some shopping anyway."

"And marshmallows," I added.

Teamwork Makes the Dream Work

As soon as my mother walked out the door, I grabbed the phone and called Ryan.

"Get over to my house ASAP!" I shouted into the phone. "Bring the gang! It's an emergency!"

Five minutes later, the doorbell rang. It was Ryan, Michael, Alexia, and Neil.

"What's up, dude?" Ryan asked. "Are you okay?"

I told them about the auction and the thousand dollars I was going to get.

"WOW," they all said, which is "MOM" upside down.

"What are you gonna do with all that money?" asked Ryan.

"I thought I might buy the Super Bowl," I said.

"I don't think the Super Bowl is for sale, A.J.," Alexia told me.

"Professor Armpit says everything has its price," I explained. "Listen, I've got a problem. I need you guys to help me make twenty more pieces of art, real fast."

"I don't know anything about art," said Neil.

"Neither do I!" I replied. "It doesn't matter! I need you to help me."

I told them Professor Armpit said I could have a one-man art show and sell my dumb art for bazillions of dollars. "If you guys help me, I'll split the money with you."

"Cool!" everybody said.

"So does anybody have an idea?" I asked.

"Nope," said Michael.

"Not me," said Alexia.

"Don't look at me," said Neil.

"Hey, have you got anything to eat in here?" Ryan asked. "I'm starved."

Ryan is always starved. He'll eat anything. I told him to see what's in the fridge.

"Hurry up," I told Ryan as he opened the door. "My mom will be home soon."

"There's a potato," Ryan said, reaching into the fridge, "and a cucumber . . ."

"Hey," said Alexia. "What if A.J. nailed the potato to the cucumber?"

"Why would he do that?" asked Neil.

"So he can put it in a museum and call it art!" said Alexia.

Hmmmmm.

"You're a genius!" I shouted. "Those art nerds will fall for *anything*!"

Alexia should get the Nobel Prize for that idea. That's a prize they give out to people who don't have bells. We went down the basement so I could get a hammer and nail the potato to the cucumber.

"There's all kinds of junk down here," said Michael. "Maybe you can make it into art."

"Yeah, anything can be art," said Ryan.

"Here's an old frying pan," said Neil.

"And here's a kazoo," said Alexia.

"Perfect!" I shouted, as I took a piece of string and tied the kazoo to the frying pan. "That's art!"

The gang was really helpful, and we created lots of cool art. We glued a stapler to a broken eggbeater. Then we attached a garden hoe to a plastic statue of Santa Claus.

"I will call this Hoe Hoe Hoe!" I said.

"You're a genius!" Ryan shouted.

When we ran out of junk down in the

basement, we went outside. The next day was garbage day, so I figured people would be throwing out lots of stuff we could use.

"You can't go poking around in people's garbage cans, A.J.," Alexia told me. "It might even be illegal."

She was probably right. Then I remembered that around the corner from my house there are some stores, and they always have a dumpster in the back.

"Follow me!" I said.

Michael, Ryan, and I climbed into the dumpster for stuff while Neil and Alexia stood guard.*

"There's *lots* of great art in here!" said

---

*Kids! Don't dumpster dive at home! This is fiction.

Michael as we rooted around in the dumpster.

"Look!" said Ryan. "A plastic funnel and a box of Jell-O!"

"That's art!" I shouted.

"Here's a busted teapot and a roll of packing tape!" said Michael.

"That's art!" I shouted.

I can't believe people threw away all this great art. We were going to make bazillions of dollars from it.

"What's this thing?" Michael asked, holding up some weird tool.

"I think it's a pickle pruner," said Alexia.

"What do you do with that?"

"You prune pickles."

"But is it art?"

"Sure it's art," I told them. "If I say it's art, it's art. I'm a genius, remember?"

Suddenly, I noticed something as I

poked my head out of the dumpster and glanced across the street.

Somebody was hiding behind a mailbox. I couldn't tell who it was, but somebody was looking at us through binoculars.

It was a spy!

The Next Big Thing

Professor Armpit had told me the art world was really fast-moving and competitive. He warned me about spies. But so what? I finished my twenty pieces of artwork over the weekend. They were ready for my big one-man show. People could spy on me all they want. Soon, I would be a bazillionaire.

The professor told me to meet him at Ella Mentry School on Monday morning, and he would take me to the gallery to set up for my art show.

I decided to do it up right. I dressed in all black. My mom got me a beret and a cape to wear.

"*Bonjour,*" I said to everybody as I glided into Miss Banks's class.

"Oh, knock it off, Arlo," said Andrea. "You don't speak French."

"Are you back at school for good, A.J.?" asked Emily.

"Oh no," I told her. "I won't be going to school anymore. I just came in to clear out my desk. Professor Armpit is picking me up for my one-man show. Then I'm going to go shopping for a speedboat. This afternoon, I might buy the Super Bowl. Do you want my autograph?"

Andrea had on her mean face. She looked really mad.

"You're a faker, Arlo!" she said. "I saw you picking garbage out of a dumpster to make your fake art."

"So it was *you* who was spying on me," I said.

"That's right," Andrea replied. "You're not a real artist. You just think you can nail two things together and pretend it's art."

"You're just jealous," I told her. I stuck

out my tongue at Andrea, and she stuck
out her tongue at me.

"I'll get you," she said.

"You and what army?" I asked her.*

I didn't care what Andrea had to say. I

_____

*Anytime somebody says, "I'll get you," just ask, "You
and what army?"

was an artistic genius, and she was just some kid who wishes she was rich and famous like me. I was going to say some more mean stuff to her, but you'll never believe who walked through the door at that moment.

Nobody! You can't walk through a door! Doors are made out of wood. Didn't we go over that in Chapter Three? But you'll never believe who walked through the door*way*.

It was Professor Armpit!

"*Bonjour*!" he announced.

Little Miss Brownnoser got all up in his face, *of course*.

"Professor Pitt," Andrea said, "may I

show you some of *my* art?"

Professor Armpit rolled his eyes.

"Is it another painting of flowers?" he
asked.

"No," Andrea replied.

"Is it cute puppies or butterflies?" he asked with a sneer.

"No."

"Well . . . okay," he said with a sigh. "I'll have a look. But be quick about it, young lady."

Andrea pointed to the ceiling. We all looked up. And you'll never believe what we saw up there.

I'm not going to tell you.

Okay, okay, I'll tell you. It was a water bottle hanging from the ceiling fan.

"How did you get that up there?" I asked Andrea.

"That's for me to know and you to find out," she replied.

"What is that, young lady?" asked Professor Armpit. "A water bottle?"

"No," Andrea replied. "It's a bottle of air. But it's not just *any* bottle of air. It's air from a specific moment in time."

"Nice try, loser!" I whispered to Andrea.

"You see," Andrea explained, "this is my environmental statement *blah blah blah blah* social commentary *blah blah blah blah* the air we breathe *blah blah blah blah* climate change *blah blah blah blah* drinking water *blah blah blah blah* drought *blah blah blah blah* points toward the sun *blah blah blah blah* . . ."

She went on and on. Professor Armpit walked around, looking at Andrea's dumb water bottle from different angles. He stared at it for a million hundred seconds.

Then he finally said, "IT'S GENIUS!"

Andrea stuck her tongue out at me.

"Do you really like it?" she asked Professor Armpit.

"I *love* it!" he replied. "You are going to be the next big thing! I'm going to make you a star!"

"Hey, what about me?" I asked. "You said *I* was going to be the next big thing."

"What's your name again?" Professor Armpit asked me.

"Artlo!" I shouted. "You named me! I created Future Art, remember?"

"Sorry, Artlo, you were the *last* big thing," he said. "That was so yesterday. The art world moves very fast, and there's

only room for one big thing at a time. This young lady is the real deal. What's your name?"

"Andrea," said Little Miss Perfect.

"From now on," said Professor Armpit, "the world will know you as . . . Artdrea!"

WHAT?!

Well, that's pretty much what happened. I guess Professor Armpit was right about the art world moving really fast. My art career was over before it even started.

I walked home from school by myself and plopped down on the couch.

"Why the long face, A.J.?" asked my mom. "What's wrong?"

"Professor Armpit doesn't like me

anymore," I told her. "He thinks Andrea is the real genius now."

I thought my mom was going to be angry, but she wasn't. She gave me a hug.

"You're not mad?" I asked. "We won't be able to get a pool now, or a new car, or build an addition on to the house."

"We didn't need any of that stuff, honey," she told me. "And we don't need you to be a famous artist. We love you just the way you are."

"Aw, thanks, Mom."

I didn't want to be an art nerd anyway.

"Now go clean up your room," my mother told me. "It's a mess."

"But, Mom, I need to have that stuff scattered all over the place so I can express my creativity."

"Nice try, A.J.," my mom said. "Go clean your room."

"Can I have some ice cream first?"

"What am I, your waitress?" she replied. "Get it yourself, A.J."

Oh, well. Maybe Professor Armpit will change his mind, and I'll be the next next big thing. Maybe people will stop sitting on babies. Maybe I'll buy the Super Bowl. Maybe an elephant will fall on Andrea's head. Maybe I should learn more French. Maybe they'll take us on a field trip to a skateboard museum. Maybe I'll get my mother a pickle pruner for her birthday. Maybe Andrea will take a class in nose blowing. Maybe people will stop holding bees and walking into doors. Maybe Ms. Hannah will make a hat out of frog turds.

But it won't be easy!

More weird books from Dan Gutman

My Weird School

My Weird School Graphic Novels

My Weirder School

My Weirdest School

 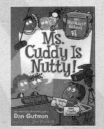

My Weirder-est School

My Weird School Fast Facts

My Weird School Daze

My Weird Tips